Book Report Bandstand
Grades 4 – 6

Written by Pamela Amick Klawitter
Illustrated by Beverly Armstrong

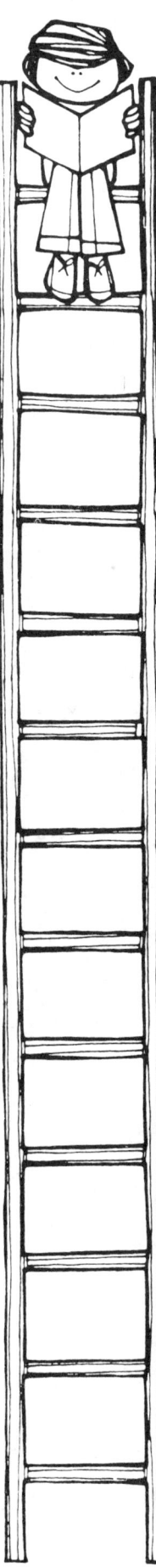

The Learning Works

Edited by Sherri M. Butterfield

The purchase of this book entitles the individual teacher to reproduce copies for use in the classroom.

The reproduction of any part for an entire school or school system or for commercial use is strictly prohibited.

No form of this work may be reproduced or transmitted or recorded without written permission from the publisher.

Copyright © 1987
THE LEARNING WORKS, INC.
P.O. Box 6187
Santa Barbara, CA 93160
All rights reserved.
Printed in the United States of America

Contents

Introduction 4

Fiction 5–26
    Anatomy of a Book 5
    Time Capsule 6
    It's News to Me! 7
    Rave Reviews 8
    TV Times 9
    Revised Edition 10
    Commercial Appeal 11
    Setting the Scene .... Setting 12
    Story Map .... Setting 13
    Character Collage .... Characters 14
    Cast Party .... Characters 15
    Who's Who? .... Characters 16
    Personal Portraits .... Characters 17
    The Plot Thickens .... Plot 18
    Nightly News .... Plot 19
    Picture This .... Plot 20
    Sum It Up .... Plot 21
    Read the Fine Print .... Details 22
    Wonder Word Search .... Details 23
    Story Cube .... Project 24
    Book-of-the-Week Award .... Project 25
    On Display .... Oral Report 26

Nonfiction 27–33
    Nonfiction Notes 27
    Let's Double-Check 28
    This Is Your Life .... Biography 29
    Pick a Place .... Travel 30
    Be a Sport .... Sports 31
    Science and Technology .... Science/Technology 32
    Step by Step .... How To 33

Miscellany 34–45
    The Play's the Thing .... Drama 34
    Designs for the Future .... Science Fiction 35
    Triple Treat .... Short Stories 36
    First Impressions .... Poetry 37
    The Way It Was .... Historical Fiction 38
    The Mystery Unfolds .... Mysteries 39
    The Wild West .... Westerns 40
    Marvelous Myths .... Myths 41
    Fabulous Fables .... Fables 42
    Terrific Tall Tales .... Tall Tales 43–44
    Amazing Animal Stories .... Animal Stories 45

Class Book Report Projects 46
Spur-of-the-Moment Book Report Ideas 47
Book Report Record 48

Introduction

Both scientific research and human experience prove that one of the most important things a child learns to do is read. A world of ideas lies at the fingertips of the child who can read for information, and the child who can read for pleasure need never be lonely or bored.

Teachers use book reports as one way of encouraging their students to read and of discovering whether or not students understand what they have read. But routine book reports—whether written or oral—can become boring!

This book contains forty-four pages of fresh ideas for book reporting activities that won't become boring. Some of these activities have been designed especially for fiction reporting, while others have been custom created for nonfiction reporting. Some of these activities are for plays and for tall tales, while others are for poems and short stories. Some of these activities help students develop critical reading skills, while others help them find new ways to enjoy what they have read. But all of these activities help students learn—and make teaching more fun!

Fiction   Name _____

Anatomy of a Book

Supply the following information about your book.

Title: _____

Author's name: _____

Illustrator's name: _____

Publisher's name: _____

Place of publication: _____

Year of publication: _____

Number of pages: _____   Number of illustrations: _____

Type of book: ___ adventure   ___ animal story   ___ fantasy

___ humor   ___ mystery   ___ science fiction   ___ sports

___ other: _____

Main characters: _____

_____

_____

Setting (time and place): _____

_____

_____

Summary of plot: _____

_____

_____

_____

Favorite part: _____

_____

How you rate this book: ___ excellent   ___ good   ___ fair   ___ poor

Book Report Bandstand
© 1987 —The Learning Works, Inc.

Fiction   Name _____

Time Capsule

A **time capsule** is a container that is filled with historical records or objects representative of current culture. It is sealed and buried or otherwise deposited for preservation. Attached to it are instructions that it be opened on some specified date or special occasion in the future.

Create a time capsule for your book. Use a container that represents something from the story. Fill it with objects that are related to events described in the book. Attach a data card that tells the title of the book, the name of the author, the name of the publisher, the year of publication, the date the capsule was prepared, and the circumstances under which it is to be opened.

Just for Fun: Do some research to learn more about time capsules. Is there one in a cornerstone or elsewhere in your town? In what other places have well-known time capsules been preserved? Has a time capsule ever been sent into space?

Fiction Name _____

It's News to Me!

A good news story answers the questions who, what, when, where, why, and how about an event. On the lines below, answer these questions about an event in the book you have just read.

Title of book: _____

Name of author: _____

Who? _____
_____

What? _____
_____

When? _____
_____

Where? _____
_____

Why? _____
_____

How? _____
_____

Just for Fun: On a separate sheet of paper, write a news story based on your answers to these six questions. In journalistic style, summarize the story in the opening sentence, which is called the **lead**, and write an appropriate headline for it.

Fiction   Name _____

Rave Reviews

A **review** is a critical evaluation of a book, motion picture, or play. Many newspapers and magazines feature reviews of recently published books. The editors of these publications hire writers to read certain books and then to write articles in which they tell what they liked about the books, what they did not like about the books, and why. Pretend that you are a reviewer for the *Daily Bugle* and have been asked to evaluate a book you recently read for this newspaper. On the lines below, summarize your review by telling what you liked about the book, what you did not like about the book, whether or not you would recommend it to other readers, and why.

Rating (circle one):   Excellent   Good   Fair   Poor
                          ★ ★ ★ ★   ★ ★ ★   ★ ★   ★

Noted book critic, _____ , has recently
                              (your full name)

finished reading _____ . In today's
                              (title of book)

edition of the *Daily Bugle*, _____ states that this
                                  (your last name)

book _____

_____

_____

_____

_____

_____

_____

_____

Fiction Name _____

TV Times

Your book has just been made into a four-part mini-series for television. *TV Times* magazine has asked you to write a brief summary for each episode. Divide the action into four sections and describe each one. Check television listings in your local newspaper for style.

Sunday PM

9:00 **4** _____
_____
_____
_____
_____
_____
_____
_____
_____

Monday PM

9:00 **4** _____
_____
_____
_____
_____
_____
_____
_____
_____

Tuesday PM

9:00 **4** _____
_____
_____
_____
_____
_____
_____
_____
_____

Wednesday PM

9:00 **4** _____
_____
_____
_____
_____
_____
_____
_____
_____

Fiction Name _____

Revised Edition

Improve upon your favorite book by doing one of the following creative writing activities. Give your revised version of the book a new title and list yourself as its author.

1. Write a new ending for the story.

2. Choose the most exciting scene in the book. Rewrite this scene by changing its setting. Keep the characters and events the same, but have them occur in a different place or time. How might this alter the outcome of the scene?

3. Allow one of the minor characters in the book to play a more important role. Rewrite one part of the story so that this character has a greater influence or effect on the outcome.

4. Rewrite your favorite part of the book using easier words so that you can read it to members of a first grade class. Do not change the main idea of the scene or the order in which the events occur. Draw and color a picture to show your listeners what is happening.

Fiction

Commercial Appeal

You have been hired by an ad agency to help boost the sales of the book you just read. On the lines below, write the script for a sixty-second television commercial outlining the major selling points of this book. Don't forget to mention both the title and the author in your script.

Fiction
Setting

Name _____

Setting the Scene

The **setting** of a book is the time and place in which the action happens. Thus, the setting is both a date or historical period and a city or countryside, real or imagined. Prepare the next reader of your book for the opening sequence of events by writing a detailed description of the setting in which these events take place.

Title: _____

Author: _____

Time: _____

_____

_____

_____

_____

Place: _____

_____

_____

_____

_____

_____

_____

KANSAS FARM CAVE CIRCUS LONDON SUBURB SWISS ALPS DESERT JUNGLE HUT MERCURY

Book Report Bandstand
© 1987—The Learning Works, Inc.

Fiction Setting

Name _____

Story Map

On a large poster board, draw a story map showing the settings in which the major events in your book take place. Depending on the story, your map might be the floor plan of a single building; the map of a city, state, or country; or the map of an imaginary land. Mark important locations on your map. Near each marked location, write a brief description indicating the major event(s) that take place there. Add a legend in which you identify and explain the symbols used on your map. And don't forget to include your name, the title of the book, and the name of its author.

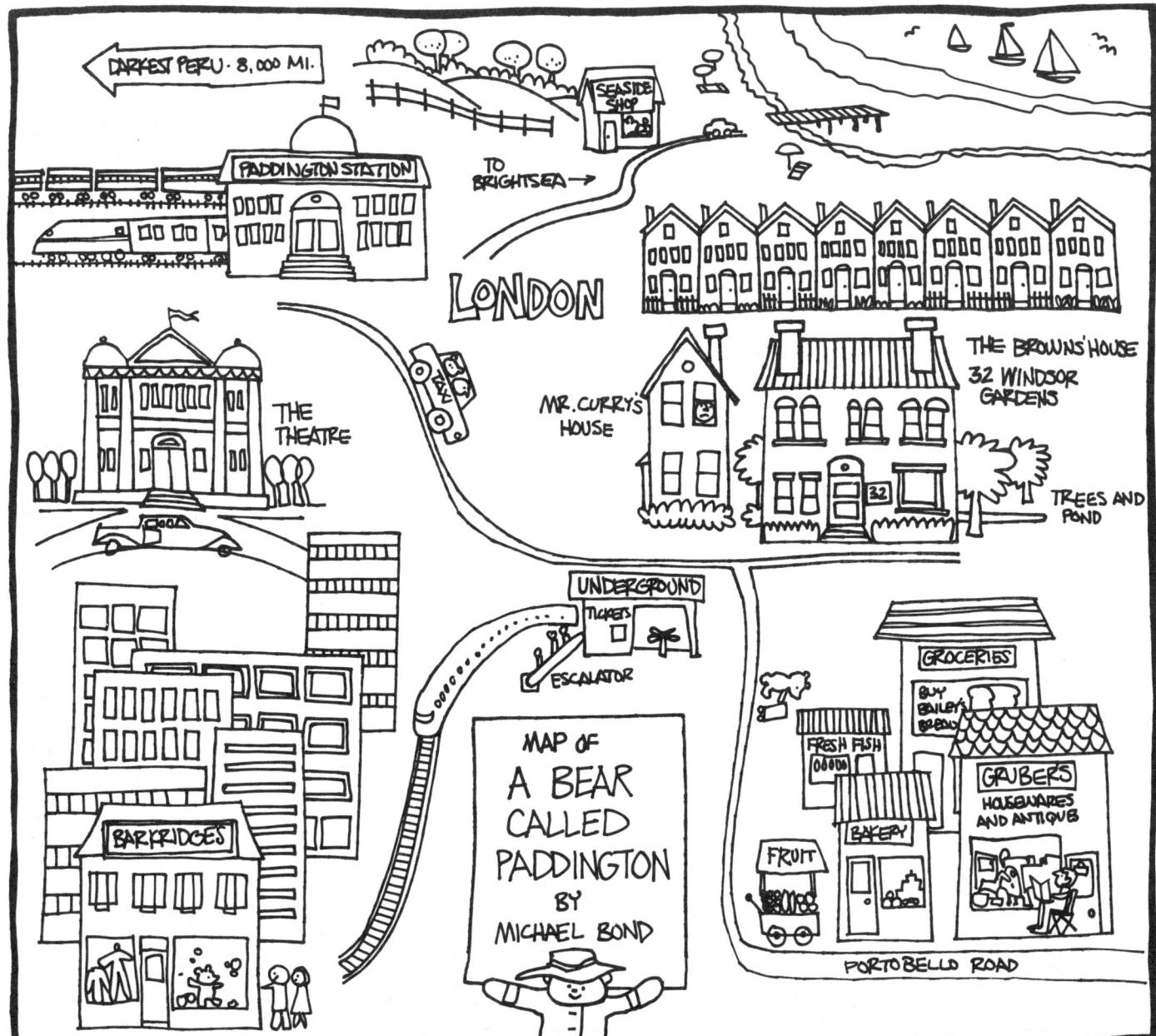

Fiction
Characters

Name _____

Character Collage

Use pictures, words, and fabric scraps to create a character collage. You will need

- one sheet of poster board
- pencil
- felt-tipped marking pens or crayons
- fabric scraps
- old magazines
- scissors
- glue
- strips of construction paper in light, bright colors

1. Using the pencil, draw a large picture of the main character from the book you have just read in the center of the poster board.

2. With crayons or marking pens, color this picture.

3. From fabric scraps, cut out and add a collar, handkerchief, hat, pocket, tie, or other similar small accents and accessories.

4. Search through old magazines to find words or phrases that describe this character and pictures that are related to him or her in some way.

5. Cut out these words, phrases, and pictures.

6. Arrange these words, phrases, and pictures around the edges of your drawing, allowing them to overlap in ways that make your composition interesting.

7. When you are satisfied with the arrangement, glue the words, phrases, and pictures in place on the poster board.

8. On one or more construction paper strips, print the title of your book, the name of its author, and your name.

9. Glue these strips in appropriate places—perhaps at the center top or center bottom—on the collage.

10. Share your character collage with other members of the class by adding it to our **Character Collage Collection**.

Fiction Characters

Cast Party

On a separate sheet of paper, plan a cast party you might give for the characters in your book. Use the steps listed below as guidelines so that you will not forget to make any important plans or arrangements. In some way, relate the party's theme to what you have read.

Title: _____

Author: _____

1. What will be the theme for your party?

2. Where and when will the party be held?

3. Describe the decorations and special effects you will use to create the mood for the party.

4. Compose a guest list for the party. Include and identify by title or role each character who has played an important part in the book.

5. Describe in detail the clothing or costume that each guest might wear.

6. Plan a menu for your party. List and/or describe the refreshments you might serve.

7. Design an invitation to the party. Include all of the information guests will need to know about time, place, and theme.

8. Plan entertainment for the party. In what games or activities will your guests participate? What music will be played?

Fiction
Characters

Name _____

Who's Who?

Pretend that the main character from the book you have just read is seeking employment and has asked you to create a resume for him or her. Match information from the book to the response categories below. Where information about the character is unknown or unavailable, write the word *unknown* on the line beside the category heading. Where a particular category is not applicable to your character, write the words *does not apply* on the line.

Name: _____ Age: _____

Address: _____

_____

Present Occupation: _____

Education and/or Special Training: _____

_____

_____

Experience: _____

_____

_____

_____

_____

Interests and/or Hobbies: _____

_____

Strong Points: _____

_____

Weak Points: _____

_____

References: _____

_____

Book Report Bandstand
© 1987—The Learning Works, Inc.

Fiction
Characters

Name _____

Personal Portraits

Characters in a book often change in one way or another as the story progresses. For example, they may change physically by naturally growing older or by being magically transformed from a human being to a monster. They may change mentally by learning or discovering something or by becoming more aware. And they may change behaviorally when something they have learned or discovered is reflected in different ways of acting and reacting. In the spaces below, draw your impression of how a character from your book looked, felt, or acted at two different times in the story.

Title of book: _____

Name of author: _____

Name of character: _____

Book Report Bandstand
© 1987—The Learning Works, Inc.

Fiction
Plot

Name _____

The Plot Thickens

In a novel or play, the **plot** is the sequence of events which makes up the story. In most books, the plot follows a predictable pattern: (1) the story begins as the setting is described and the characters are introduced; (2) the problem is described; (3) the action intensifies, or rises, as the characters attempt to solve the problem; (4) the action reaches a climax that determines whether or not the problem will be solved; (5) the action becomes less intense, or falls; and (6) the story ends, often with some hint of how the solution of the problem will affect the characters in the future. Outline the plot of your book by describing each of these six parts on the lines below. If you need additional space, use the back of this page or a separate sheet of paper.

Title of book: _____

Name of author: _____

Type of book: _____

1. Introduction: _____
   _____

2. Crisis or problem: _____
   _____

3. Rising action: _____
   _____

4. Climax: _____
   _____

5. Falling action: _____
   _____

6. Resolution: _____
   _____

PLOT PLOT PLOT PLOT

Fiction
Plot

Name _____

Nightly News

Headlines are words that appear in large, dark type above a news story and tell what the story is about. A **lead** is the opening paragraph of a news story. It is usually one sentence and no more than thirty words in length. A good lead summarizes the story by telling who, what, when, where, and sometimes how and why about the newsworthy event that forms the basis of the story. From the book you have just read, choose three important events. For each event, write a headline and a lead.

Example

Headline: Mysterious Disappearance Rocks City

Lead: The city was stunned today by news of the sudden and unexpected disappearance of local amateur detective, Nancy Drew.

Title of Book: _____

Name of Author: _____

First Event

Headline: _____

Lead: _____

_____

Second Event

Headline: _____

Lead: _____

Third Event

Headline: _____

Lead: _____

_____

Book Report Bandstand
© 1987—The Learning Works, Inc.

Fiction
Plot

Name _____

Picture This

Remember those picture books you liked to look at when you were younger? They had few if any printed words and relied, instead, on drawings or photographs to tell their stories. Choose one of your favorite picture books. Write the title of this book and the name of its author on the lines below. Then, retell its story by creating a word picture to go with the illustrations.

Title: _____

Author: _____

_____
_____
_____
_____
_____
_____
_____
_____
_____
_____

Butterflies drifted past daisies

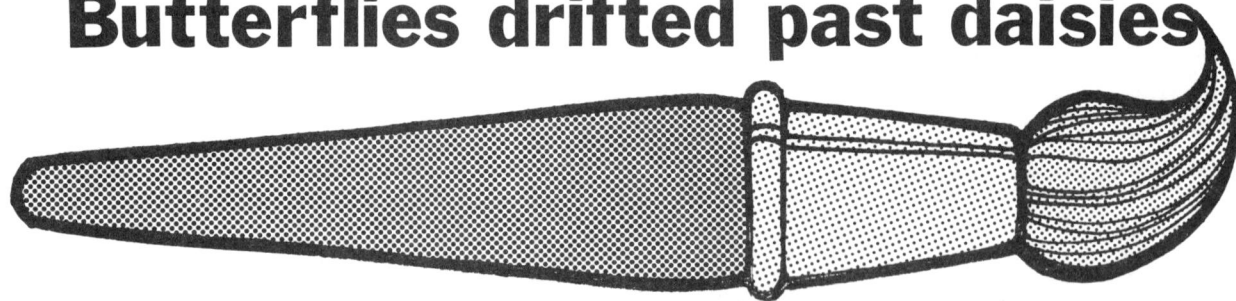

Just for Fun: Select a story that has been or can be told in a few sentences. Turn this story into a picture book by creating a series of illustrations for it.

Fiction
Plot

Name _____

Sum It Up

First, write the title of the book you have just read and the name of its author on the lines below. Next, choose your five favorite chapters and record the numbers and titles of these chapters. If the chapters don't have titles, make up ones you feel would be appropriate. Then, summarize the main idea of each chapter in one or two sentences.

Title of book: _____

Name of author: _____

Chapter number and title: _____
_____
_____
_____

Chapter number and title: _____
_____
_____
_____

Chapter number and title: _____
_____
_____
_____

Chapter number and title: _____
_____
_____
_____

Chapter number and title: _____
_____
_____
_____

Fiction Details Name _____

Read the Fine Print

How well do you read for details? First, write the title of the book you have just read and the name of its author on the lines below. Then, find and copy seven sentences from this book which provide the details to answer each one of these questions. Also record the number of the page on which you find each sentence.

Title of book: _____

Name of author: _____

1. Where does the story begin? _____ . Page ___

2. When does the story begin? _____ . Page ___

3. What are the first and last names of the main character? _____ . Page ___

4. How does the main character look? _____ . Page ___

5. What is the weather like at some point in the story? _____ . Page ___

6. How does the main character feel at some point in the story? _____ . Page ___

7. How does the story end? _____ . Page ___

Fiction Details

Name _____

Wonder Word Search

Make your friends wonder with a word search based on the book you have just read. First, write the title of the book and the name of its author on the lines provided. Second, choose the words you will use. Consider the author's last name, the characters' first names, a word or two from the book title, place-names that are important to the story, and objects that are mentioned in the book. Third, write the words you choose in alphabetical order on the numbered lines below. Next, arrange these words in the puzzle spaces by printing them in capital letters from left to right, from right to left, from top to bottom, from bottom to top, and diagonally. Then, print letters in the blank spaces of the puzzle grid to hide these words. Finally, make copies of your puzzle and challenge some of your friends to search for the hidden words.

Title of Book: _____

Name of Author: _____

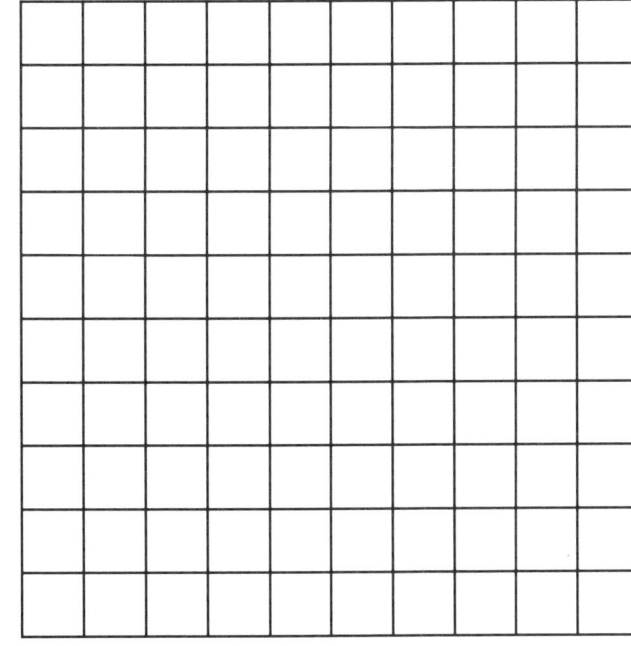

1. _____   6. _____
2. _____   7. _____
3. _____   8. _____
4. _____   9. _____
5. _____   10. _____

Book Report Bandstand
© 1987—The Learning Works, Inc.

Fiction
Project

Name _____

Story Cube

Three-dimensional book reports make an eye-catching display when placed side by side on a classroom bookshelf or table or when stacked along a wall or in an otherwise bare corner. To make one, you will need

- a cardboard box that is cubical and measures at least 12 inches square
- enough butcher paper, shelf paper, wallpaper, or wrapping paper to cover the box
- old magazines
- at least three sheets of writing paper
- a pencil or writing pen
- felt-tipped marking pens
- tape
- glue
- scissors

1. Tape the top and bottom of the box closed.

2. Cover the closed box with paper.

3. Using a felt-tipped marking pen, label three sides of the box **setting**, **plot**, and **characters**.

4. On the fourth side, print the title of the book and the name of its author.

5. On separate sheets of paper, write three paragraphs in which you describe the setting of the story (both time and place), the plot (events that happen in the story), and the characters.

6. Glue each one of these descriptions to the appropriate side of the box.

7. From old magazines, cut pictures that depict characters, events, feelings, ideas, objects, or places from the story.

8. Glue these pictures to the top and bottom of your box so that they create colorful montages.

9. Display your completed story cube in your classroom.

Fiction Project

Name _____

Book-of-the-Week Award

Congratulations! Your book has been nominated for the Book-of-the-Week Award. Complete the following activities in time for the awards ceremony.

Title of Book: _____

Name of Author: _____

1. Design an appropriate award for the contest winner. It can be something traditional—like a ribbon, medal, trophy, or cup—or it can be something unusual that has been especially designed to depict a theme from the book.

2. Prepare a brief acceptance speech to be given at the ceremony. In this speech, mention the reasons you feel the book is worthy of this award.

3. Write a letter to the contest judges from the main character in the book or from its author thanking them for considering and selecting your book.

4. Design a poster illustrating important scenes or themes from your book. Include both the title of the book and the name of its author. This poster will become part of a permanent display in the Book Report Hall of Fame.

Fiction
Oral Report

Name _____

On Display

1. Assemble a collection of objects that are somehow related to the plot of your book.

2. For each object, create a three-inch-by-five-inch label card by writing (a) the name of the object, (b) the name of the character in the book to whom this object belonged, and (c) a brief explanation of the object's significance in the story.

3. To accompany your display, design a poster that includes the title of the book, the name of the author, and an illustration depicting the theme of the story.

4. Display your poster and labeled objects on a desk or table where your classmates will have an opportunity to enjoy them.

5. Create a simple costume that will transform you into one of the characters in your book.

6. Dressed as this character, give a brief narration of the story, using the objects in your display as cues.

Nonfiction   Name _____

Nonfiction Notes

Supply the following information about your book.

Title: _____

Author's name: _____

Illustrator's name: _____

Publisher's name: _____

Place of publication: _____

Year of publication: _____

Number of pages: _____   Number of illustrations: _____

Type of book: ___ biography   ___ collections   ___ crafts, models
___ history   ___ hobbies   ___ how to   ___ science   ___ sports
___ other: _____

Subject area: _____ Call number: _____

Reason you chose this book: _____
_____

Eight interesting facts you learned from this book:

1. _____
2. _____
3. _____
4. _____
5. _____
6. _____
7. _____
8. _____

How you rate this book: ___ excellent   ___ good   ___ fair   ___ poor

Nonfiction Name _____

Let's Double-Check

A nonfiction book is supposed to provide its reader with factual information about a particular person or topic. But how can you be certain that the information in a nonfiction book you read is factual? How can you verify its accuracy? Do some detective work to double-check the facts in a nonfiction book you have read recently.

Title of Book: _____

Name of Author: _____

Name of Publisher: _____

Year of Publication: _____

1. Choose ten facts from your book which you would like to double-check.

2. Print each fact on a separate three-inch-by-five-inch index card. On the same side of the card, write the name of the author, the title of the book, the date of its publication, and the number of the page on which you found the information you are double-checking.

3. Use an up-to-date encyclopedia or other reference book to double-check each fact.

4. On the other side of each fact card, record the information as it appears in the reference book. Include the name of the reference book, the date of its publication, the number of the page on which you found the information, and whether it is the same as the information found in your first source or differs from it.

5. If the information found in the two books differs, look up the same information in a third source to see if you can determine which is right and which is wrong.

6. Place your ten fact cards in an envelope.

7. On the front of the envelope, print the title of the book, the name of the author, and your name.

8. If some of the information in your book differs from the information you found in other sources, include a card on which you offer one or more possible reasons for these differences. Consider, for example, the years in which the books were published and the relative expertise of the authors who wrote them.

Book Report Bandstand
© 1987—The Learning Works, Inc.

Nonfiction
Biography

Name _____

This Is Your Life

The English word *biography* comes from two Greek words, *bios*, meaning "life," and *graphein*, meaning "to write." Thus, a **biography** is a written account of a person's life. A biography is written by one person about another person. An **autobiography** is written by one person about himself or herself. Read a biography or autobiography about a famous person. Write the title of the book and the name of the author on the lines. Then, complete one or more of the activities described below.

Title: _____

Author: _____

1. Use the facts you have learned to write an encyclopedia entry about the person. Before you begin writing, read through several entries in your classroom encyclopedia to familiarize yourself with the style that is used for entries of this kind.

2. Create a diary that might have been written by the person about whom you have just read. Write at least five dated entries based on some of the outstanding events in this person's life.

3. Make an illustrated time line that includes each of the important dates mentioned in the book. Obtain three three-inch-by-five-inch plain index cards for each date. On one card, write the date with a dark, felt-tipped marking pen. On the second card, name or describe the event. On the third card, draw a picture to show what happened. Punch one hole in the center top and one hole in the center bottom of each card. String the cards together with yarn in chronological sequence.

Book Report Bandstand
© 1987 — The Learning Works, Inc.

Nonfiction
Travel

Name _____

Pick a Place

Read a book about an exotic place or foreign country. Then, design a travel pack that will convince a friend to visit this destination.

Title of book: _____

Name of author: _____

Destination: _____

1. On an outline map, draw the route your friend will follow to get from your hometown to the chosen destination.

2. Along the route, add small pictures to show each means of transportation your friend will use.

3. Make a separate ticket for each one of these means of transportation.

4. Fold an 8 1/2-inch-by-14-inch piece of white paper in thirds.

5. Turn the folded paper into a brochure by adding words and pictures that highlight the most characteristic and/or unusual features of the destination. Include factual information about major points of interest.

6. Design, make, and decorate a pocket folder.

7. Place the map, tickets, and brochure in the folder.

8. Fasten the folder closed with a brad, string, or yarn.

9. Display your completed travel pack in our **Pick a Place** center.

Nonfiction
Sports

Name _____

Be a Sport

Use this form to report on a book you have read about your favorite sport.

Title of book: _____

Name of author: _____

Name of sport: _____

How is this sport played? _____

_____

_____

_____

_____

What special equipment is used or worn to play this sport?

_____

_____

List the names and describe the accomplishments of some of the athletes who have been especially good at this sport.

_____

_____

_____

_____

What is your opinion of this book? _____

_____

_____

Nonfiction
Science/Technology

Name _____

Science and Technology

Use this form to report on a book you have read about some aspect of science and/or technology.

Title of book: _____

Name of author: _____

Why did you choose this book? _____
_____

What specific field or area of science or technology is discussed or explained in it?
_____

What did you hope to discover or learn by reading it? _____
_____
_____

List six facts you learned by reading this book.

1. _____
2. _____
3. _____
4. _____
5. _____
6. _____

List ten words you added to your vocabulary by reading this book.

1. _____   6. _____
2. _____   7. _____
3. _____   8. _____
4. _____   9. _____
5. _____   10. _____

Nonfiction
How To

Name _____

Step by Step

First, read a book that tells how to do something. Then, on the lines below, list the materials that are needed and describe the steps one should follow to complete this process or project. If you need additional space, continue on the back of this page or on a separate sheet of paper.

Title of book: _____

Name of author: _____

This book tells how to_____.

Materials needed:

_____   _____

_____   _____

_____   _____

_____   _____

Steps to follow:

1. _____

   _____

2. _____

   _____

3. _____

   _____

4. _____

   _____

5. _____

   _____

6. _____

| 1 | 2 | 3 | 4 | 5 | 6 | 7 | 8 | 9 | 10 | 11 | 12 | 13 | 14 | 15 | 16 |

Book Report Bandstand
© 1987—The Learning Works, Inc.

Miscellany
Drama

Name _____

The Play's the Thing

First, choose and read a play. Then, use this form to report on it.

Title: _____

Playwright: _____

Who is the main character in the play? _____

What are the names of some of the supporting characters?

_____   _____

_____   _____

What is the primary goal of the main character? _____

_____

What prevents him or her from achieving this goal? _____

_____

What does he or she do to overcome this obstacle? _____

_____

_____

Does the main character achieve his or her primary goal? _____

Explain your answer to this question. _____

_____

How does the ending of this play make you feel? _____

_____

Just for Fun: A television program that tells a story, or a small part of a story, is actually a kind of play. It is a **screenplay**, that is, a story that has been written in dramatized form and is intended to be photographed and shown on a screen. Watch an episode of your favorite television series and answer these same questions about it.

Miscellany
Science Fiction

Name _____

Designs for the Future

Science fiction is fiction that deals with how real or imagined science affects people. Science fiction stories are usually set in another place and time, often in a technological world of the future. Read a science fiction book. Then, in the four spaces below, sketch pictures of things you might find in a future world. Base your sketches on descriptions contained in the book.

Title of Book: _____

Name of Author: _____

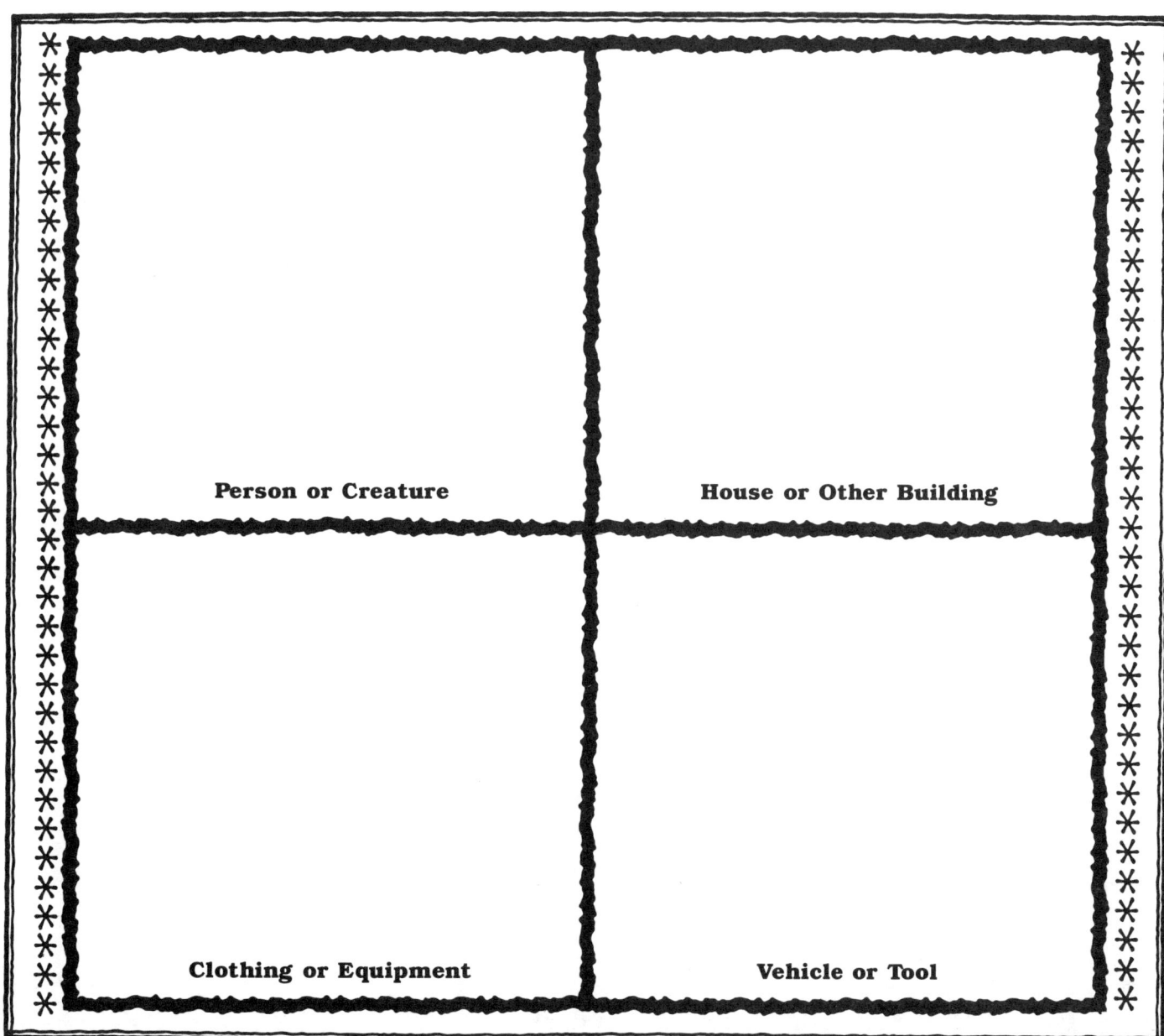

Person or Creature

House or Other Building

Clothing or Equipment

Vehicle or Tool

Book Report Bandstand
© 1987—The Learning Works, Inc.

Miscellany
Short Stories

Name _____

Triple Treat

    First, read three short stories by the same author. Second, write the name of the author and the titles of these stories on the lines below. Then, briefly summarize each one of these stories. Finally, on the back of this page or on a separate sheet of paper, write a paragraph in which you compare these three stories. Describe the ways in which they are similar and the ways in which they are different. Then offer some possible reasons or explanations for these similarities and differences.

Name of Author: _____

First Story

Title: _____

Summary: _____

_____

_____

_____

Second Story

Title: _____

Summary: _____

_____

_____

_____

Third Story

Title: _____

Summary: _____

_____

_____

_____

Miscellany
Poetry

Name _____

First Impressions

After you have read a collection of poems, choose your favorite poem and complete the activity described below. To do so, you will need

- one 12-inch-by-18-inch sheet of construction paper
- two sheets of writing paper cut to measure approximately 5 inches by 10 inches
- one sheet of drawing paper also cut to measure approximately 5 inches by 10 inches
- a pencil or writing pen
- crayons or felt-tipped marking pens
- glue

1. Fold the sheet of construction paper in thirds so that it is divided into three rectangular panels.

2. Copy your favorite poem on one sheet of writing paper in your very best handwriting. Don't forget to include the title of the poem and the name of the poet who wrote it.

3. Glue this poem to the middle panel of the folded paper.

4. On the sheet of drawing paper, create a picture that illustrates what this poem means to you.

5. Glue this picture to the left-hand panel of the folded construction paper.

6. On the other sheet of writing paper, summarize the meaning of the poem in your own words. Don't forget to sign your name.

7. Glue this summary to the right-hand panel of the folded construction paper.

8. Unite the three panels by adding a border or some other decorative motif.

Book Report Bandstand
© 1987 —The Learning Works, Inc.

Miscellany
Historical Fiction

Name _____

The Way It Was

Read a fiction book for which the setting is a different period in history. In this book, find three specific examples of how some areas of life—for example, buildings, clothing, communication, education, food, recreation, or transportation—have changed from that period to this. In the middle column of the table below, record one area of life for each number. In the right-hand column, describe what this area was like then and what it is like now in a manner that illustrates the degree of change or the amount of difference.

Title of Book: _____

Name of Author: _____

Historical Period: _____

	Area of Life	Description
1		**Then**
		Now
2		**Then**
		Now
3		**Then**
		Now

Miscellany
Mysteries

Name _____

The Mystery Unfolds

A **mystery** is a story dealing with the solution of a problem or a crime. In a well-written mystery, the author presents a series of facts, or **clues**, that lead to the solution. First, read a mystery. Second, on the lines below, write the title of the book and the name of its author. Next, list five important clues that are presented as the mystery unfolds. If possible, include some clues that are ambiguous. Then offer two possible explanations or solutions that are compatible with the clues you have listed. Finally, challenge a friend to read the clues and choose the correct solution.

Title of Book: _____

Name of Author: _____

1. _____
2. _____
3. _____
4. _____
5. _____

Solution 1: _____

Solution 2: _____

Miscellany
Westerns

Name _____

The Wild West

A **western** is a story, book, motion picture, or radio or television program about life in the western part of the United States during the second half of the nineteenth century. First, read a book about the Old West. Second, record the title of this book and the name of its author on the lines provided. Then, in the space below, create a wanted poster for the villain in this book.

Title: _____

Author: _____

WANTED

Name: _____

Aliases (if any): _____

Description: _____

_____

Identifying Marks: _____

Dastardly Deeds: _____

_____

Favorite Means of Transportation: _____

Places Villain Has Previously Hidden, Lived, or Visited: _____

_____

Friends or Family Members with Whom Villain May Seek Refuge: _____

_____

Person to Contact If Villain Is Seen: _____

Miscellany
Myths

Name _____

Marvelous Myths

First, read one myth from each of two different countries or cultures. Next, use this sheet to record information about these myths. Then, on separate sheets of paper, draw pictures of the main characters from each myth. Finally, punch holes in this sheet and in your pictures, and add them to our **Classroom Mythology Notebook**.

First Myth

Title: _____

Country or culture: _____

Main character(s): _____

_____

_____

Problems character(s) face: _____

_____

_____

Second Myth

Title: _____

Country or culture: _____

Main character(s): _____

_____

_____

Problems character(s) face: _____

_____

_____

Book Report Bandstand
© 1987—The Learning Works, Inc.

Miscellany — Fables

Name _____

Fabulous Fables

A **fable** is a story that is made up to teach a lesson. The lesson taught by a fable is called a **moral**. After reading several fables, choose the one you like best and write a modern version of it. Change the characters, setting, and language to reflect today's society. Give your fable a new title. Describe the main point of the story in a one-sentence moral at the end.

Original Title: _____

Author (if known): _____

New Title: _____

_____
_____
_____
_____
_____
_____
_____
_____
_____
_____
_____

Moral: _____
_____

Miscellany
Tall Tales

Name _____

Terrific Tall Tales

Tall tales are stories in which details are exaggerated and the truth is stretched for humorous effect. These stories were first told in America during the nineteenth century. To entertain one another, pioneers made up stories about a logger named Paul Bunyan, a cowboy named Pecos Bill, a railroad engineer named Casey Jones, a "steel drivin' man" named John Henry, and other folk heroes. Read several tall tales about the same hero. Choose one of these tales. Record the title of this tale on the line below. Then, use this tale to complete the activities on pages 43 and 44.

Title: _____

1. Give one specific example of exaggerations in the descriptions of each of the following story elements:

   a. The setting: _____
   _____
   _____

   b. A character: _____
   _____
   _____

   c. An everyday object: _____
   _____
   _____

Book Report Bandstand
© 1987—The Learning Works, Inc.

Terrific Tall Tales
(continued)

2. The tellers of tall tales often exaggerate measurements (for example, distances, heights, weights, and sizes). Write an example of this kind of exaggeration from your story on the lines below.

   _____
   _____
   _____

3. The tellers of tall tales sometimes use unbelievably large numbers and amounts. Write an example of the use of this technique in your story on the lines below.

   _____
   _____
   _____

Just for Fun: Select one of the exaggerations you noted in either item 1, 2, or 3 and illustrate it on a separate sheet of paper.

Miscellany
Animal Stories

Name _____

Amazing Animal Stories

Animal stories are stories in which the main characters are animals. There are at least three types of animal stories: fantastic, realistic, and scientific. An **animal fantasy** is an animal story in which the animals act like people. They talk, experience human emotions, and may even wear clothes. **Realistic animal stories** are a form of fiction, but they are true to life. The animals in these stories don't talk or wear clothes. Instead, they behave as animals normally do. **Scientific animal stories** are nonfiction and recount the actual observations and experiences of people who have lived and worked closely with animals. Read an animal story. In the spaces below, draw a four-frame comic strip based on some event in the lives of the animals described in this book.

Title of Book: _____

Name of Author: _____

1	2
3	4

Book Report Bandstand
© 1987—The Learning Works, Inc.

Name _____

Class Book Report Projects

1. Use construction paper strips or yarn to turn a classroom bulletin board into a series of "bookshelves" to be filled with construction paper "spines" representing all of the books that have been read by each member or the class. On each spine, write the title of the book, the name of its author, and the name of the student who has read it.

2. Fill a bulletin board with **Friendly Fictitious Faces**. Provide drawing paper cut in circles or ovals and suggest that each student draw the face of the main character in a book he or she has read. As you post each face on the bulletin board, add an index card on which are printed the character's name, the book title, the author's name, and the student's name.

3. Create a **Ready Reference File of Student Book Reviews with Ratings**. Use three-inch-by-five-inch index cards and follow a format similar to this one.

```
Author:_____
Title: _____
Type of book: _____
Number of pages: _____
Brief summary: _____
_____
_____
Comments:_____
_____
Rating:     Excellent   Good   Fair   Poor
Reviewer: _____
```

4. Hold a class book swap. With parents' permission, have students bring to class all of the old paperback books they have read and trade them for books they have not read. Swap could be run as an auction during which students give brief sales pitches about their books to get other students interested in reading them.

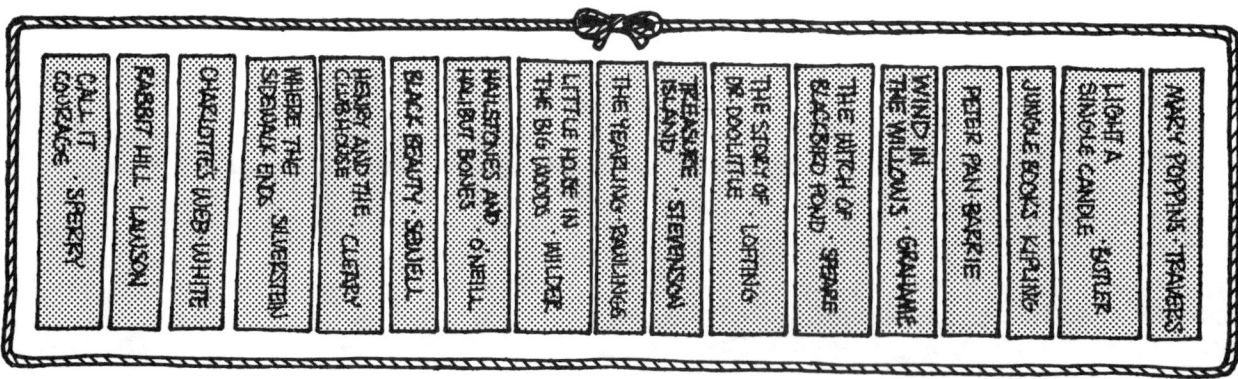

Book Report Bandstand
© 1987—The Learning Works, Inc.

Name _____

Spur-of-the-Moment Book Report Ideas

1. Design a new dust jacket for the book. Look at several to familiarize yourself with the information that should be presented on the jacket.

2. Design a poster to advertise the book.

3. Write a poem about the book.

4. Create a comic strip based on one chapter or one character in the book.

5. Write a tall tale or fable based on several events in the book.

6. Develop your four favorite parts of the book into a short play.

7. Write a letter to a newspaper advice columnist from the main character in the book asking how to solve some problem he or she faces.

8. Write a letter to the author telling him or her what you liked or did not like about the book.

9. Write a brief biography of one of the main characters in the book. Base it on information found in the story.

10. Create a puppet to represent your favorite character in the book.

11. Construct a diorama to illustrate your favorite part of the book.

12. Keep a log of new words that you encounter in the book. Beside each word write its part of speech, its pronunciation, and its meaning.

13. Make a list of ten questions for which the answers can be learned by reading the book.

14. Read a book about something you are studying in school. Compare the information found in your reading book with the information found in your textbook. In what ways are they similar? In what ways are they different? What factors might account for the differences you have observed?

15. Tape record yourself reading a chapter from the book. Add appropriate sound effects as you go along.

16. Tape record a staged interview between a famous book critic and the author or main character of the book. Play the role of the interviewer and the interviewee yourself or write a script and ask a friend to play one of these roles while you play the other.

Book Report Bandstand
© 1987—The Learning Works, Inc.

Name _____

Book Report Record

Title	Author	Date of Report	Grade on Report

Book Report Bandstand
© 1987—The Learning Works, Inc.